CLONE
CHAOS

A TEMPLAR BOOK

First published in 2011 by Templar Publishing,
an imprint of The Templar Company Limited,
The Granary, North Street,
Dorking, Surrey, RH4 1DN, UK
www.templarco.co.uk

copyright © 2011 by Simon Bartram

First edition

All rights reserved

ISBN 978-1-84877-032-4

Designed by Mike Jolley
Edited by Anne Finnis

Printed in the United Kingdom

BOB & BARRY'S LUNAR ADVENTURES

CLONE CHAOS

SIMON BARTRAM

templar publishing
www.templarco.co.uk

IDENTITY CARD

Name: **Bob**

Occupation: **Man on the Moon**

Licence to drive: **space rocket**

Planet of residence: **Earth**

Alien activity: **unaware**

W.A.A.

WORLDWIDE ASTRONAUTS' ASSOCIATION

CHAPTER ONE

"PICKLED ONIONS!" said Bob, the Man on the Moon, as his rocket approached Earth. "Whatever I do, I mustn't forget the pickled onions!!!"

Bob's shopping list was a little shorter than usual. Because Barry, his unusual six-legged dog, had gone away for a while, there was no need to buy bone-shaped biscuits or flea powder. Just lately, Barry had started to whiff a little and Bob had decided that a short spell at the swish new Poodle Parlour on Pluto would do his best-ever friend the world of good. Of course, life without him was a tad lonely but at least when Barry returned he wouldn't stink out the rocket.

Having safely landed at the Lunar Hill launch-pad, Bob quickly changed into his Earth clothes and cycled into town. Luckily, he just caught Seamus Typhoon's General Store and Post Office before it closed. Along with the pickled onions, he put six packets of football stickers, a smallish bag of plums and a plastic comb into his shopping basket before rushing to the till.

The shopkeeper, Seamus Typhoon, seemed very surprised to see him. "More pickled onions?" he remarked. "That's the second jumbo jar you've bought in the last fifteen minutes. You'll begin to look like a pickled onion if you're not careful!"

Bob was puzzled. "I think you're confusing me with someone else," he said politely as he paid and left. "Next stop, Home Sweet Home!" Bob smiled, looking forward to savouring his speciality – 'PICKLEDY ONIONY SOUPY SUPPER' – in front of the big match.

That evening, however, his home didn't seem so sweet. As he walked up the garden path, he noticed the dark silhouette of a figure through the drawn curtains of the kitchen window.

"H... HOLY HELMETS!" he thought. "IS THAT A... A... A... BURGLAR?!!!"

Bravely, he opened the front door and tippy-toed up the hallway to get a closer look. A tall, slim, red-haired man was standing with his back to Bob, emptying a jumbo jar of pickled onions into a bubbling pan. Bob hardly dared breathe for fear of alerting the intruder.

But he was outraged by what he saw. This frightful chap had helped himself to Bob's tea and gingerbread astronauts. He'd raided the fridge and the cupboards and even discovered the secret stash of dry-roasted peanuts hidden inside the old hot-water bottle. His feet were cosily snuggled into Bob's slippers as they tapped away to the delightful drones of Bob's favourite bagpipes CD. And, to top it all, the intruder had the nerve to be wearing Bob's favourite, limited edition 'Eclipse of the Sun' commemorative tank top.

"WHAT A RIGHT ROYAL CHEEK!" blurted Bob, momentarily losing his cool. The startled intruder suddenly swivelled around. Bob's eyes widened and his jaw dropped. He couldn't believe what he was looking at. There, standing

as plain as day, in front of him was... HIMSELF!!!
Or at least, a perfectly exact copy of himself from
the top of his quiff to the tips of his toes.

Bob was astounded and terrified at the same
time. Oddly, the intruder-impostor was gaping at
Bob as if BOB was the intruder-impostor. Bob
screamed and made a frantic beeline for the
front door, only to find the intruder-impostor

making exactly the same frantic beeline right alongside him.

Worse still, Bob then found his escape route blocked by a second big surprise. Two large, strange-looking men filled the doorway. They were snazzily kitted out in shiny silver boiler suits and white face masks that covered their noses and mouths. If Bob hadn't known better he would have sworn it was Halloween. However, these sinister visitors had no interest in sweetie treats. They were intent only on playing a dastardly trick. And what a trick it was! Without uttering a word they each raised an arm and pointed, one directly at Bob and one at the impostor. Then, from two tiny holes in the forefingers of their gloves, a misty green vapour jetted out and Bob became overwhelmed with wooziness. His legs began to wobble under the weight of his heavy eyelids as the hallway was lost under a thick pea-soupy fog...

A few seconds later, after two dull thuds, the silver men stepped into the house and re-emerged carrying two sleeping bodies. They carefully placed them into the back of an unmarked van and drove off into the moonlit night as, all around, the hoots of owls warned of trouble.

CHAPTER TWO

Bob's sleep was as deep and dark as a starless universe. Only his own booming snores eventually woke him with a start. As he groggily rubbed the sleep from his eyes, Bob was bamboozled to find himself sitting in a velvety seat in a small, deserted theatre. Even stranger, to his right his own very distinctive snoring continued. With a sense of foreboding he turned his head and there, in the very next seat, was the looky-likey impostor, sleeping like a baby. Automatically, Bob screamed, which woke the impostor who saw Bob and screamed right back. For a second time they scrambled to make their escape, but the heavy doors were locked.

Keeping a safe distance from him, Bob stared at the impostor.

"St… stay away!" he shouted. "I'm… I'm… t… tougher than I look!"

The impostor, whose voice seemed identical to Bob's, sounded just as flustered.

"S… s… so am I!" he stuttered.

Finally, after a few tense minutes, their stand off was ended when the Head of the Department for Moon Affairs, Tarantula Van Trumpet, walked in, pushing a rattling tea trolley.

"Gentlemen, gentlemen," he said sharply. "You two chaps should be friends. Trust me, you've got a lot in common. Now, sit down

and have some tea. There are important things you need to know."

Bob's surprise at seeing Tarantula and his fear of the impostor were both outweighed by his desire for a nice cup of tea.

The impostor agreed and so, cautiously, they both sat down to drink and listen.

"Firstly," said Tarantula, "I'm sorry-ish for the way in which you were brought here, but it was essential for security purposes. You are sitting in a secret conference theatre, burrowed deep into the Earth below the headquarters for the entire Universe, Infinity House. Now, I have a short piece of film for you to watch."

The lights dimmed. A big screen descended from the ceiling and somewhere behind them a projector began to roll. Of course, Bob loved a good blockbuster, but somehow he wasn't expecting a Western. He was right.

The film began with famous genius scientist

Professor Gertrude Sickle standing in a gleaming laboratory. Next to her was a strange machine on which dancing dials and ticking gauges surrounded a heavy metal door with a porthole in it. Steam hissed from the machine's pipes. From her pocket Professor Sickle produced a ten pence piece and popped it into a small slot before pulling a long, golden lever. This triggered some kind of electrical storm within the now violently vibrating machine. Through the porthole, crackling forks of lightning exploded amongst flashing strobe lights. Faster and faster the steam hissed from the juddering pipes until soon the entire machine was just a murky blur within the wild swirls. The whole laboratory was rattling. The din was deafening. It was breathtaking.

And then, suddenly, the commotion stopped. An eerie silence replaced it. Gripping the arms of his seat, Bob could just about make out the door of the machine swinging open. Then, slowly, a

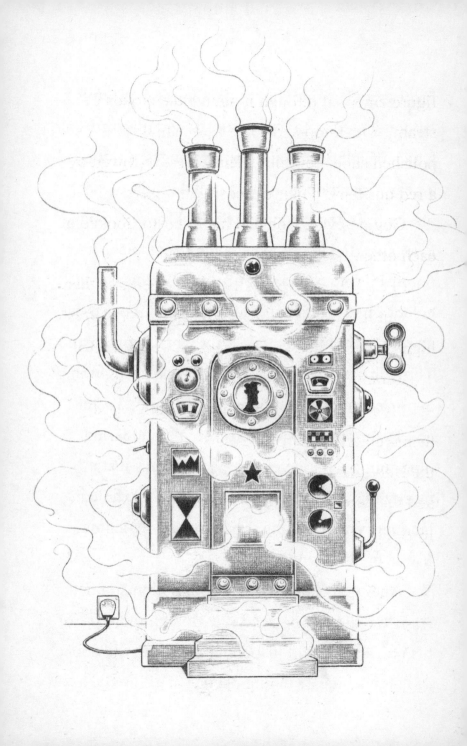

figure emerged through it amidst the clouds of steam. A tank top and some astonishingly polished shoes revealed themselves, followed by a red quiff and a pair of sensible trousers.

Goggle-eyed, Bob and his impostor looked at each other.

"IT… IT… CAN'T BE!" they cried together.

But it was. Sure enough, standing six metres high on the silver screen was ANOTHER BOB!

Tarantula paused the film.

"It's all quite simple," he said, looking at them coolly. "One of you is
the Bob in the film
and that Bob…
IS A CLONE!!!"

CHAPTER THREE

Luckily, Tarantula Van Trumpet's teapot was not yet empty. He quickly poured two strong cups of tea and passed them to Bob and the impostor, who were both close to fainting.

Consulting the mini pocket dictionary that had come free with his cornflakes, Bob double-checked the meaning of the word clone. It was described as being 'an absolutely, completely and utterly, spot-on accurate, tip-top copy of another living thing'. To Bob that sounded like science fiction, but, as he stared at the impostor, he quickly realised that it was actually science fact.

Tarantula did his best to explain the situation:

"During a most pleasant chat with Santa at last year's Christmas party," he said, "I happened to mention that the Moon was in terrific shape. It was cleaner than ever before and the Moon tourist numbers had rocketed upwards. I said how well Bob was doing and that we could do with another just like him in case he was ever poorly or on holiday or missing in action. Then the Moon would always be looked after, no matter what! Professor Sickle was there. Her ears pricked up.

'Leave it to me!' she shouted.

Six months later she returned with her Clonemaster 4000, the machine in the film. Having programmed into it the DNA information found in a single strand of Bob's hair, Professor Sickle succeeded in creating a perfect copy of the Man on the Moon. It looked the same and sounded the same. It had the same likes and dislikes and the same strengths and weaknesses. It was, and of course is, so accurate that even now, as we sit here, one of you has no idea that he is a clone."

Bob and the impostor looked at each other.

"WELL, IT'S NOT ME!!" they both shouted at the same time.

"I was at home," added the impostor, "making soup! And well before HE arrived!"

Bob was peeved. "That's because," he retorted, "I spent the afternoon where the Man on the Moon should have been – ON THE MOON!!! And I have definitely never, EVER, been inside that Clonemaster thingy!"

"Well, neither have I!" argued the impostor. "I would have remembered if I had!!"

Tarantula shook his head. "Not necessarily," he said. "You see, for a while after creation, the Bob clone's brain would have been terribly hazy. Professor Sickle assures me that it wouldn't remember those first few hours. When finally its memory did kick in, it would only remember ordinary, everyday Bob memories. And er... by that time it had escaped."

"Escaped?" said the Bobs.

"Yes! I'm afraid I rather foolishly let the clone pay a visit to the loo on its own and it ended up walking straight out of Infinity House. The security guard, Norbert Shortbread, knew nothing of the secret experiments. He just thought it was Bob on his way home after a bog-standard Moon meeting."

"And so you sent the silver men to bring it back?" asked Bob.

"Of course," replied Tarantula, "we had tests and studies to carry out. We couldn't leave the greatest advance in the history of science to wander around willy-nilly. What if it had been hit by a minibus or fallen down a manhole? The big problem now though was that the Man on the Moon shift was over. By the time our men caught up with the clone there were two Bobs at home. They hadn't the foggiest which was which and, until we can carry out some tests, neither do we! For the sake of the Moon we really MUST find out who the real Bob is!"

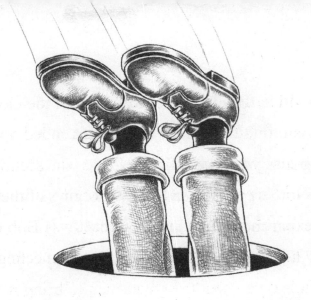

Bob was becoming frustrated.

"I'M THE ONE TRUE BOB," he shouted. "Why should I have to be poked and prodded just to prove it?"

The impostor was equally miffed.

"DITTO!" he snapped.

Tarantula was unmoved.

"Until this matter has been resolved," he calmly continued, "Norbert Shortbread is under strict instructions not to let you leave. Tonight you will be made comfortable and tomorrow our work to find the real Man on the Moon will begin."

Tarantula then led his 'guests' out of the theatre and into their uncertain futures.

Bob was very cheesed off.

"I'm no clone," he mumbled under his breath.

The impostor mumbled right back.

"DITTO again," he said.

CHAPTER FOUR

Even though Bob had been to Infinity House many times he still only knew the foyer, the lift and the inside of Tarantula Van Trumpet's brown office on the seventeenth floor. It came as quite a surprise to discover that there was a great big bunker burrowed beneath the main skyscraper. He was told it had originally been built in the olden days to be a secret hideaway for Infinity House officials, should the dreaded alien invasion of Earth ever occur.

"What a hoot!" thought Bob. "Just how people could have believed in such alien clap-trap I will never know!!"

The bunker was now home to the DEFENDERS OF THE NOBLE UNIVERSE TASKFORCE or 'DONUT' for short. DONUT had been set up to be a cosmic Secret Service intended to solve all manner of hush-hush space problems. In fact, the silver men despatched to Bob's door were both high ranking DONUT agents. In the bunker canteen Tarantula introduced them as Bunny Withers and Columbo Hutch, and they were delighted when Bob and the impostor gratefully accepted a 'no hard feelings' fairy cake each.

En route to their dormitory for the night, the Bobs were escorted through a maze of corridors. The bunker was incredible. There was a hi-tech gym, an Olympic-sized swimming pool, two rocket simulation pods and even a state-of-the-art bingo hall that doubled up as a disco every Tuesday afternoon.

Inside the deserted dormitory a pair of bunk beds had been prepared. On each Saturn-patterned duvet cover a pair of pyjamas had been laid out along with a toothbrush, bed socks and a sachet of cocoa. Ordinarily, it would have been a rather pleasant place to spend a night or two. However, one huge problem was bothering Bob: while he was being tested who'd take care of the Moon? As well as the next day being crater-count Wednesday, there were SIX tour rockets booked to visit. Without him to keep order, the tourists would run the risk of tripping headlong into a crater or forgetting to poopy-scoop up after their dogs.

"And there's that tea stain near Crater 573 to scrub again," thought the impostor out loud. "Sam said that it's still noticeable even from Saturn."

Bob was puzzled. "How do *you* know about that tea stain?" he asked.

"Because," replied the impostor, "I AM BOB – THE MAN ON THE MOON!! I spilled the tea as I was giggling uncontrollably at that tourist's hilarious space chimp impression."

Despite his outrage at the impostor's claims,
Bob's identical brain recalled the same memory
and he couldn't help but chuckle. For a few
seconds they laughed together. The ice had been
broken. Nervously, the impostor jumped down
from the top bunk and held out his hand. Bob

shook it. For now they agreed that the only thing that mattered was escaping to their beloved Moon. Unfortunately, no ingenious escape plans sprang to mind and so they decided to sleep on it. Wearily, they put on their pyjamas before popping to the vast DONUT bathroom to clean their teeth. The shower cubicles were packed with DONUT agents following their weekly pea-shooting practice. Vigorously, the Bobs brushed away whilst attempting to check their quiffs in the steamed-up mirrors. Using paper towels, they wiped away the condensation. And that's when they noticed something glinting over their shoulders. Minty-mouthed, they turned around and their eyes landed upon two silver boiler suits complete with space masks hanging by the lockers.

"Are you thinking what I'm thinking?" asked the impostor.

"We'd only be borrowing them," responded Bob thoughtfully.

Five minutes later, the lift pinged open in the foyer of Infinity House and two silver men in face masks stepped out and made for the exit. Norbert Shortbread was glued to the big match on a tiny TV perched on the reception desk.

"Off on some more important spacey business, lads?" he asked.

Coolly, the silver men nodded once and then walked out into the bright moonlight. Their clever disguises had worked. Bob and the impostor had escaped.

CHAPTER FIVE

Bob's plan was simple. Get to the Moon, carry
on as normal and hide in the craters should any
DONUT agents come sniffing about. Of course, he
would have much preferred to have been travelling
alone, but the impostor clone was having none of it.
Therefore, for the sake of keeping the peace, Bob
kept his lips zipped.

Having hitched a lift on Toni Vanilla's ice
cream van, the two Bobs soon safely arrived at
the Lunar Hill launch-pad. In preparation for take
off, they each did three star jumps and a squat
thrust before urgently swapping their silvery suits
for two Man on the Moon spacesuits. Having

drawn the short straw, Bob was slightly miffed to have to wear the old suit with the small tear in the seat of the pants but again he didn't complain. There were more important things to worry about. The shrill, ear-splitting sound of a siren had suddenly filled the night, scattering owls from their trees.

"They know we've escaped!" cried Bob. "We haven't much time!"

Rapidly they clambered aboard Bob's trusty rocket and, with Bob in the pilot seat, blasted spacewards. The closer they flew to the Moon the larger it grew and gradually, a peaceful calm descended over the cockpit.

Unhappily, it wasn't to last. Without warning, the rocket violently jarred to a halt in mid-space as if it had smashed into an almighty invisible wall. Then, some kind of mysterious force began to pull them backwards, away from the Moon. Bob's rear-view mirror explained everything.

No fewer than TEN powerful DONUT rockets were TOWING the Bobs back to Earth. Skilfully, they had each cast a rope with a super-strength magnet attached, and each of those magnets had clamped onto Bob's rocket. They didn't stand a chance and so Bob calmly turned off the engine, sat back and, in harmony with the impostor, sang sad space shanties as the Moon shrank away. For now, at least, it would have to look after itself.

Back at Infinity House, Bob was expecting to be greeted by a sour-faced Tarantula Van Trumpet, but, in fact, it was a sour-faced Norbert Shortbread who appeared.

"Mr Van Trumpet is stuck in the toilet again," he snapped, "and so I have been entrusted to escort you back to your dormitory. This time I am

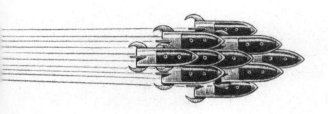

NOT going to let him down. Now, you two follow me and NO MORE SHENANIGANS!"

Too tired to argue, Bob and the impostor followed Norbert back into the secret heart of the bunker. They were eventually led to a door with a sign that read 'Dormitory Two'.

"Weren't we in Dormitory One last time?" whispered Bob. The impostor nodded.

Inside, the dormitory was almost pitch black. Just a table lamp illuminated their bunk beds which, once again, had pyjamas laid out upon them. All around, booming snores bounced off the walls. The dormitory seemed full.

Wearily, Bob changed and climbed into bed before drifting off into a moonless sleep. However, after only a few dozing minutes, he woke with a start. A livid Tarantula was ranting at Norbert Shortbread in the corridor outside.

"YOU WEREN'T SUPPOSED TO PUT THEM IN THAT DORMITORY, YOU NINCOMPOOP!" he bawled. "YOU WERE SUPPOSED TO KEEP THEM SEPARATE FROM THE REST! NOW THEY'RE ALL MIXED UP!!"

The whole of the dormitory began to stir. Bob could hear mumbling voices that he vaguely recognised. A bedside lamp clicked on, followed

by another and another until the whole room was
aglow. Rows of bunk beds stretched the length of
the walls and in each one there seemed to be a
red-haired man stretching and yawning. Bob

rubbed his groggy eyes and looked more closely.
He couldn't believe what he was looking at. In
each and every bed, as plain as the nose on his
face, was… A BOB!!!!

CHAPTER SIX

It was turning out to be a most unusual night. After ducking under his duvet in panic, Bob eventually poked his head out again to find his bed surrounded by smiling clones.

"You must be Bob!" said one of them. "My name is Bob. This here is Bob. That there is Bob. He's Bob and he's Bob. They're all Bob and the chap who's just popped out to the loo is Bob. We haven't the faintest idea what's going on but we're a great bunch o' lads."

"We all like fancy teapots," said a second clone.

"And support the same football team!" added a third.

"We don't like prunes, though," warned a fourth, looking serious.

It was hard for Bob not to warm to his new 'friends' as they chatted and chuckled until morning when a frazzled-looking Tarantula Van Trumpet traipsed in.

"Hello, gentlemen," he said sheepishly, before speaking at length about Professor Sickle, her Clonemaster 4000 and the events of the previous twenty-four hours. "Having created our one desired clone," he explained, "the Clonemaster's 'OFF' button became well and truly stuck and we couldn't stop the unwanted clones streaming out of the machine. It wasn't until late last night that we realised we could simply unplug it at the wall. By that time, however, we had created no fewer than ninety-nine Men on the Moon.

"Worse still, last night two Bobs were accidentally placed into this dormitory. One of

them is the real Bob. He is amongst you now but we have no idea how to pinpoint him. Our terrible meddling has proved to be disastrous. The Moon is without its Man."

Bob's hand shot up into the air. "IT'S ME!" he shouted. "I'M THE ONE TRUE BOB!!"

Around him, however, ninety-nine other hands had also been urgently raised.

"I'M THE ONE YOU'RE LOOKING FOR!!" bellowed one clone.

"NO! OVER HERE!" yelled another. "I'M HIM, REALLY!"

In that split second, Bob's affection for the clones evaporated. A terrible worry gripped him. Undoubtedly, he was the one true Bob, but how could he prove it? Each and every clone was staggeringly accurate, right down to the minuscule Eiffel-Tower-shaped birthmark hidden behind their left ears.

"If I can't tell myself apart from the clones," he fretted, "then what hope has Mr Van Trumpet got?"

Bob knew that it was essential that he didn't panic and he remained focused.

"I must remember at all times who I am! I'm Bob – the Man on the Moon!! The truth will out, I KNOW IT WILL!!"

Tarantula was also trying to look confident. "Don't worry, gentlemen," he declared. "I WILL find a way of identifying the real Bob. To that end, I must insist that each one of you remains here."

Groans and moans filled the dormitory.

"You can't keep me away from the Moon!!" shouted a clone.

"There's vital vacuuming to be done," complained another.

The grumbling increased when Tarantula revealed that substitute spaceman, Les, the Man on Nowhere in Particular, had been drafted in to look after the Moon. Les was lazy and unkempt and Bob, along with the clones, was appalled. It got worse. To buy himself some time, Tarantula had fibbed to Moon fans everywhere.

"The public thinks that Bob has chicken pox," he said, "and so the Moon tourists will not be surprised when he is not there!"

The groans now reached fever pitch but, before a riotous rebellion could break out, the dormitory door was dramatically flung open and bright lights flooded the room. Even Tarantula was stunned.

Standing there, accompanied by a ravenous pack of reporters, photographers and camera crews, was Professor Sickle.

"CHICKEN POX POPPYCOCK!!!" she screamed. "NO-ONE COVERS UP MY WORK OF GENIUS!"

Then, as the press swamped the dormitory, mayhem erupted and Bob and the clones were completely overwhelmed. At the same time, a few floors above, Norbert Shortbread's mini-TV was broadcasting the chaotic scene live and at the bottom of the screen a yellow, rolling caption read: 'BREAKING NEWS – SECRET MAN ON THE MOON CLONES DISCOVERED!'

CHAPTER
SEVEN

Later that day, as the sun went down, Bob, along
with seven cramped clones, blasted upwards from
Earth in his super-fast rocket. As it whooshed
over Infinity House, he noticed a grey-faced
Tarantula gazing out of his seventeenth-floor
window sipping a cup of tea. Following the
arrival of the world's press, Tarantula knew it was
pointless to keep Bob and the clones hidden away
in the bunker. The secret was well and truly out.
Therefore, reluctantly, he'd instructed Norbert
Shortbread to let them leave for the Moon, which
was already struggling to shine through the night

sky. At least somewhere amongst all the clones Bob would be on hand to give the Moon the love it needed. Tarantula, meanwhile, would have peace and quiet to work out exactly who was the real Bob.

Until then, Bob would, of course, have to endure the company of ninety-nine pesky hangers-on. His rocket was flanked by a fleet of lunar taxis and stella shuttle buses that were ferrying the other clones Moonwards, each one convinced that he was numero uno.

Despite this, Bob was determined that life should return to normal as quickly as possible and, as his rocket zoomed closer to his favourite place in the universe, his heart looped the loop with excitement. On arrival, though, it very nearly shattered at the shocking sight that greeted him.

Somehow, within the space of a day, Les, the Man on Nowhere in Particular, had transformed Bob's glowing Moon into a tatty tip lost under a blanket of banana skins, crisp packets and cans.

Immediately, a sneeze shot out of his nose,
tickled out by a swirly fog of dust. All around
him the clones were atishooing, too, as were
many poor tourists who had fallen into deep
craters and been abandoned by the uncaring Les,
who was snoring in a deckchair. Bob was stunned.
Nothing was just so, or tip-top, or even tickety-boo.

Over the coming days there would be much work to do. In theory, Bob thought that the moon should have been spic-and-span one hundred times quicker than if he'd been working alone. In practice, though, it was chaos.

During the weekly crater count, for example, each one of the Bobs was determined to be heard above the others. Amidst the resulting babbled jumble of numbers, an irritated Bob found it impossible to reach twenty without losing count.

Simple cleaning and tidying became troublesome too. The over-polished surface of the Moon became dangerously slippy and Bob's vintage hoover exploded through overuse!

Everywhere he turned, the clones were in Bob's way. They competed fiercely with him for the Moon-tourists' attention. If Bob was performing a sensitive Moon-mime, a clone would attempt to distract his audience with ridiculous space chimp impressions or perhaps an upbeat karaoke number.

Bob quickly realised that he was going to have a battle on his hands to come out on top. His rivalry with the clones became terribly intense. Nothing else seemed to matter. Incredibly, he even began neglecting Health and Safety, and several tourists suffered bouncy castle mishaps or were knocked over by the miniature train on loan from Neptune. In time, the visitors stopped coming. The Moon just wasn't such a fun place to be anymore.

On Earth, Bob's home life wasn't any happier. With only twelve of them able to fit into the bedroom, the other eighty-eight had to settle in the garage, the shed or the tree house. More than once, Bob was forced to spend the night shivering in Barry's kennel.

Each day Bob began to leave the

Moon earlier and earlier on the space hopperbus in a bid to seize the evening newspaper or be the first in the queue to use the nose-hair scissors. But every one of the clones had the same idea.

And then, one terrible day, they were all so busy arguing over the last teabag that they forgot to go to the Moon altogether! Bob was truly horrified. It was the wake-up call he needed. Selfishly, he'd been thinking only of himself. He didn't deserve the honour of being the Man on the Moon. In the midst of the clones, he wept and the clones wept with him as the same terrible thought began to creep into their brains.

"Maybe I... I... I'm NOT the one true Bob," whimpered one of them.

"Perhaps I AM just a clone?" worried another.

Bob was sure of only one thing. "It's time to end this nonsense," he said. And then, right on cue, the telephone rang. Excitedly, Tarantula Van Trumpet shouted his news over the speakerphone.

"I'VE DONE IT!" he cheered. "I KNOW HOW TO FIND THE REAL BOB!!!"

CHAPTER
EIGHT

"PINK BLANCMANGE AND SWEETCORN!"
declared Tarantula, "those were the ingredients
we needed to cook up an answer to our problem!"

Sitting in the DONUT Apollo shuttle pod,
awaiting blast-off, Bob and the clones were still
none the wiser. Tarantula was standing at the
front of the cabin.

"I HAD to find out if the Clonemaster 4000
was as accurate as it appeared to be," he explained.
"I needed a clone AND its original to pinpoint a
way of finding any differences. The simplest thing
to do was to clone myself, as a test case!"

At that moment the shuttle pod's cockpit door swung open and a familiar figure emerged carrying a bulging book.

"Gentlemen," declared Tarantula, "I would like you to meet… MR TARANTULA VAN TRUMPET!!" The Bobs gasped as the clone greeted them.

"Being me," continued Tarantula, "my clone quickly grasped the seriousness of the situation and during the following days we lived, worked and played together. We built model ships. We baked cakes. We pot-holed. We spent many a happy hour waltzing around the ballrooms of the town. However, I couldn't find a single difference between us. What hope then could I possibly have had of finding a difference between the one true Bob and his clones? But, finally, one Saturday supper time I had a breakthrough. Having enjoyed our gammon and pineapple Mrs Van Trumpet presented us both with a magnificent spotted dick for dessert. 'The custard's on its way,' she said. And that was when my clone astounded me. 'Could I have pink blancmange instead?' he asked. Well, I very nearly fell off my chair. All my life I have loathed pink blancmange with a passion. I was cock-a-hoop."

"Excitedly, I rushed to Infinity House and programmed this incredible information into our top computer. Its flashing calculations lifted my heart. There was a one per cent difference between myself and my clone!! THE CLONEMASTER 4000 DID NOT PRODUCE A PERFECT CLONE AFTER ALL!! Therefore, all we must do is find that magnificent difference in all but one of you. The Bob in which we can find no variation will be the real Man on the Moon!"

Bob and the clones tried to be enthusiastic but something was puzzling them. Bob spoke for all. "But surely, if you aren't certain who the original is, you'll have nothing to compare the others to?"

Tarantula was unfazed. He beckoned his own clone, took the bulging book from him and held it aloft like a trophy.

"Who needs the original Bob when we've got THIS?" he cheered. "It's an extraordinarily detailed super-scrapbook that contains every teeny tiny morsel of information about Bob. The whole thing was

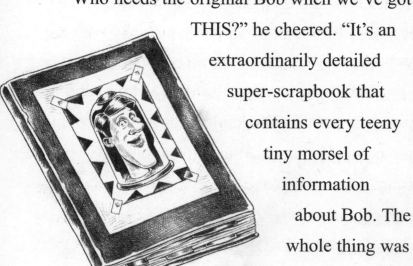

painstakingly compiled by eight-year-old Charlie Sweetcorn, who sent it to us in the hope of getting it signed by his hero, the Man on the Moon. Using it as a guide I have devised a series of Bob tests, the results of which will be compared to the information on these pages. Any Bob whose results deviate, even slightly, from it is not the real Bob and can be automatically eliminated from the running!"

Tarantula and his clone then strapped themselves into their seats. "Gentlemen," concluded Tarantula, "I'm delighted to have you on board. On your beloved Moon a surprise awaits you. In the meantime sit back and relax. You're going to need the rest!"

Relaxing, however, would prove to be impossible. Bob felt nervous. What if he somehow failed a test? What if Charlie Sweetcorn's super-scrapbook wasn't accurate? What if one of the pesky clones decided to cheat?

His brain was overloading and it wasn't helped when, as the shuttle pod approached the Moon, his saucer-sized eyes spied Tarantula's surprise. There, on the lunar surface, glinting in the starlight, was a colossal coliseum!

Tarantula was beaming. "That's where the tests are going to happen," he said, smiling at them. "Bobs, take a moment to focus your minds. IT'S CRUNCH TIME!!"

CHAPTER NINE

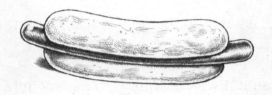

From day one Professor Sickle had been
determined to earn her fortune from the clones.
On hearing about Tarantula's tests, she steamed
right in and turned what should have been a
straightforward scientific experiment into a
money-spinning showbiz extravaganza. Literally
overnight the Moon was transformed. It crawled
with TV crews. There were souvenir stalls and
hot dog vans. Flags waved and horns blew.
Constructed from a flat-pack kit, the awe-inspiring
coliseum could have sold out ten times over.
Even the normally grumpy-ish Tarantula couldn't
hide his excitement.

To tell them apart, Bob and the clones were each allocated a number and a snazzy, patterned spacesuit unique to them. Though Bob was disappointed to be number eleven instead of number one, he was delighted to have been handed a smart red and white striped spacesuit that closely resembled the kit of his favourite football team. As he changed into it, butterflies swirled around his tummy. The clones looked equally nervous. Like jittery gladiators, their legs wobbled as they were led out into the buzzing arena where Tarantula addressed the crowd. He informed them of the importance of Charlie Sweetcorn's super-scrapbook.

"Ninety-nine of the Bobs," he explained, "will NOT correspond exactly to the Bob documented in its pages. They may be lankier, or loopier, or lazier and so on. Only one will be an absolute tip-top match and HE will be our one true Man on the Moon."

So, from the VIP box, as special guest Charlie Sweetcorn kicked off the proceedings. "Let the games begin!!" he proudly pronounced. And begin they did, with a 'LOOKY LIKEY CHALLENGE ROUND' during which the Bobs were closely studied and compared to hundreds of drawings and photos in the super-scrapbook. Two competitors crashed out at this first hurdle. Clone-Bob 72 had six extra nose-hairs and Clone-Bob 57's minuscule birthmark looked less like the Eiffel Tower and more like the Blackpool Tower. Surprised and teary, they were banished to the stands.

Next was 'THE SOUVENIR AND SNACK STALL INSPECTION ROUND'. Each Bob was given a small table on which to arrange his spacey knick-knacks, trinkets and nibbles in the hope of selling them to a panel of judges posing as Moon tourists. Several more clones bit the dust. Incredibly, Clone-Bob 12 not only failed to make chit-chat with his customers, but he didn't

have one single chocolate-covered nut on sale. It
was a glaring mistake. Bob was amazed. For him,
though, it was so far, so good. He was quietly
confident. The truth will out, he thought.

During the following hours the competition
hotted up with vacuuming duels, space shanty

sing-offs and mini pork pie gift-wrapping exercises. Sensationally, Clone-Bob 21 was disqualified for sneaking a peak at the super-scrapbook. Then Clone-Bob 33 surprised everyone by voluntarily dropping out to pursue his dream of working in a carpet shop. Eventually, after some epic lunar battles, only Bob and Clone-Bob 92 remained to compete in the final event, 'THE BLINDFOLDED MARATHON SPRINT'. Bob stared at his very last opponent.

"If that crucial difference is in him," Bob thought, "then it must be buried way down in the depths of his being." He could feel his confidence beginning to wane as he and Clone-Bob 92 were transported by moon buggy twenty-six miles away from the coliseum. They were then blindfolded, spun around three times and left to find their way back to the arena using the moon maps imprinted on their brains. The winner of this race would be crowned the one true Bob.

Skilfully, they slalomed past deep craters, devilish crevices and perilous plateaus. One led and then the other. They stumbled and collided. Their routes parted and converged. Pluckily, they huffed and puffed and panted until, neck and neck, they re-entered the coliseum and crossed the finishing line without a sliver of moonlight between them. The crowd gasped. Tarantula was bamboozled. It was deadlock.

Bob was losing faith in the truth. "WHAT ON EARTH ARE WE GOING TO DO NOW?" he thought desperately.

CHAPTER TEN

After forking out £1.50 for a ticket plus 90p for the Lunar Bus, the fans in the coliseum would certainly NOT have been happy to leave without knowing who the one true Bob was. Kindly, to give Tarantula time to think, the clones agreed to entertain the restless crowd. They were still, after all, ninety-nine per cent Bob, and Bob was always happy to help. So, cheerfully they put on a short play about the birth of the universe, followed by a forty-nine a-side football match in which Clone-Bob 50 was spotted and signed up by a talent scout from Spanish champions, Real Barthelonia.

While all this was going on, nobody noticed Bob suddenly spring up and whisper something in Tarantula's ear. No one witnessed Tarantula's emergency flying saucer spiriting away towards Pluto. And not a single soul spotted it return half an hour later, with an extra passenger onboard. Tarantula was ready.

As the clones returned to their seats the coliseum floodlights suddenly went out and were replaced by a powerful spotlight that illuminated the two remaining Bobs. They were standing in the centre of the arena. Then a second spotlight lit up a trapdoor in the arena floor a few metres away from them. It was slowly opening and something was climbing up the steps from the darkness below. The crowd murmured. In row seventeen Fernando Fandango panicked. "TARANTULA IS RELEASING THE LIONS!!" he yelped. "THE BOB THEY EAT LAST WILL BE THE WINNER!!!"

Immediately, the murmurs turned to screams that became louder when a head cautiously peeped out through the trapdoor. However, it wasn't the head of a lion. It was the head of a dog – an awfully unusual, very familiar dog! IT WAS BARRY... BOB'S BEST-EVER FRIEND!!!

The crowd wowed as he timidly stepped into the arena smelling of roses and looking like a million dollars. Straight away his eye landed on the two Bobs. Barry almost fainted with confusion. The crowd was transfixed.

"GENIUS!!!" concluded Tinkerbell Privet. "TARANTULA'S USING BARRY TO SNIFF OUT THE ONE TRUE BOB!!"

Barry's trembling gaze darted between his two potential masters. He stared into their eyes. He sniffed their aromas. He sensed their souls. And suddenly he knew. Excitedly, he ran faster than a train, straight as a die, past Clone-Bob 92 and leapt gleefully into the arms of... BOB!!

The crowd erupted. Streamers flew and confetti fell. Soon Tarantula emerged, with the weight of the universe lifted from his shoulders. "BEHOLD, THE ONE TRUE BOB!!" he declared.

As the crowd cheered again, Bob felt an overwhelming rush of happiness. Clone-Bob 92, on the other hand, looked less than chuffed.

"HOLD YOUR HORSES!!!" he cried, "THIS IS A TRAVESTY OF JUSTICE!! MY PERSONALITY PERFECTLY CORRESPONDS TO THE SUPER-SCRAPBOOK TOO!! YOU CAN'T JUST GO CHANGING THE RULES WILLY-NILLY!!"

The smile fell from Bob's face.

"But look at the dog!" implored Tarantula, "he would surely know his own master, wouldn't he?"

"TOTAL BUNKEM!" snapped Clone-Bob 92, "YOU CAN'T SERIOUSLY LEAVE SUCH A GINORMOUS DECISION TO A SIX-LEGGED ALIEN MUTT?!!"

And that was when, just for a split second, the cosmos stopped ticking. 300,000 intakes of breath left the coliseum silent until eventually a giggle wiggled out from Bob's mouth.

"Hee, hee, haa," he chortled. "He... he... said that Barry was... an... an... ALIEN DOG!!!! AHHAAAAARAAHAHAHAA!!!"

Never had he heard anything so ridiculous. His laughter was infectious. Quickly it spread across the coliseum. Everyone knew that the one true Bob did not, no way, no how, believe in aliens. Clone-Bob 92 obviously did!! Tarantula didn't need to consult the super-scrapbook. Clone-Bob 92's one per cent difference had blatantly revealed itself. Even he *himself* knew he was defeated and, having shaken his opponent's hand, he slowly trooped off to the stands to join the other clones.

When Bob finally managed to stop laughing, Tarantula once again introduced him as the one true Bob. Then having swiftly changed into his beloved white suit, Bob began a triumphant lap of honour with Barry. Streamers flew and confetti fell. The truth had prevailed.

And that was that. Along with Charlie Sweetcorn and his signed super-scrapbook, the fans departed for Earth with smiles on their faces. Slightly sadder, the clones left too. Each though, would enjoy an amazing life – from Clone-Bob 33 who would own the 'COSMIC CARPET SUPERSTORE' chain, to Bob the Impostor, who would star in over fifty Hollywood blockbusters.

As for Professor Sickle, she ditched the world of science to try and cash in on the clones' achievements. One by one, however, the clones ditched her and she ended up a lonely old woman in a poky flat with a miserable cat.

And as for Bob, life returned to the same old humdrum affair it had been before all of the clone chaos... and he loved it. With Barry at his side, Bob could once again simply be the undisputed, hundred per cent genuine, one true Man on the Moon.

THE END?

THE END